ANGEROUS
GAMES
TRAPPED

Sue Graves

Rising Stars UK Ltd.
7 Hatchers Mews, Bermondsey Street, London SE1 3GS
www.risingstars-uk.com

 nasen

NASEN House, 4/5 Amber Business Village, Amber Close,
Amington, Tamworth, Staffordshire B77 4RP

Published 2012

Author: Sue Graves
Series editor: Sasha Morton
Text and logo design: pentacor**big**
Typesetting: Geoff Rayner, Bag of Badgers
Cover design: Lon Chan
Publisher: Gill Budgell
Project Manager: Sasha Morton Creative Project Management
Editorial: Deborah Kespert
Artwork: Colour: Lon Chan / B&W: Paul Loudon

British Library Cataloguing in Publication Data.
A CIP record for this book is available from the British Library.

ISBN: 978-0-85769-614-4

Printed by Craftprint International, Singapore

CHAPTER 1

It was Tom's birthday.

"Happy birthday, Tom," said Kojo. He handed Tom a large card. "This is from me and Sima."

"Yes, happy birthday, Tom," said Sima. "Hope you like it."

Sima, Tom and Kojo worked at Dangerous Games, a computer games company. Sima designed the games, Kojo programmed them and Tom tested them. They worked as a team and they were all good mates.

Tom ripped open the envelope and pulled out the card.

"Cool!" he said. "Thanks, guys."

"Look inside, Tom," said Sima. "You'll love it."

Tom opened the card. Inside was a voucher for Tom to go potholing on Saturday.

"Oh, wow!" he said. "I've always wanted to go potholing."

"You get proper tuition from an expert potholer," said Sima. "Then he takes you down into all these caves, so you can see what it's really like."

"And we want to hear all about it when you get back," said Kojo.

"Why don't you come with me on Saturday?" asked Tom. "After my potholing session, we could meet up at Frankie's Café for lunch and I can tell you all about it."

"Why not?" said Sima. "As long as you don't bore us to death — I'm not sure potholing will hold my attention for too long!"

CHAPTER 2

On Saturday morning, Tom went to the potholing centre. There were lots of people there and Tom met Ben, the potholing expert.

Ben showed Tom what he had to wear to go potholing. He explained how to keep safe underground. It was really interesting.

Then Ben took Tom deep underground into the caves. It was amazing. The roofs of the caves were very low and there were narrow tunnels and passageways leading off from the main caves. Often Tom and Ben had to crawl on their stomachs to move through the tunnels. Tom thought it was brilliant.

Later that morning, Tom met up with Sima and Kojo at Frankie's Café.

"How did it go?" asked Kojo.

"It was the best experience ever," said Tom. He ordered a coffee and a sandwich and pulled up a chair. "Ben was a really good instructor and he told me a lot about the caves. He even told me about this scarily deep cavern called the Bone Bowl."

"Yuk!" said Sima with a shiver. "I don't like the sound of that."

Tom laughed. "No, I agree, it was a bit gruesome," he said. "Apparently the Bone Bowl got its name years ago when three potholers died trying to explore it. No one has ever tried again."

On Monday, Tom was still talking about his potholing experience.

"I tell you," he said. "You ought to try it for yourselves. It's amazing."

Sima looked thoughtful. "Is potholing really popular?" she asked.

"Well, if it's not, it should be," said Tom.

"Hmm ..." said Sima. "Then I think I might have an idea for a new game."

Soon Sima had worked out the designs for the new game.

"It's based on a scavenger hunt," she explained to the boys. "The players have to check items off a list while they are potholing."

"What sort of things do they have to find?" asked Kojo.

"Things like animal bones, fossils and pieces of ore," said Sima.

"And what about stalactites and stalagmites?" suggested Tom.

"Ooh yes, good idea," said Sima. She made a note on her plans to include Tom's suggestions. "All I need now are some photographs of the caves to scan in to create the graphics for the game."

"I can help you there," said Tom. He pulled out his wallet and took out some photos. "There was a photographer at the centre when I went potholing. He gave me these as a souvenir."

Sima looked through the photos. "These are great," she said. "Who are these people?"

She pointed to the two men standing by Tom in one of the photos.

"Jed and Ryan," said Tom. "They were really cool. They were in the same caving session as me."

Sima took the photos and scanned them into her designs. Then she gave the designs to Kojo and he programmed the game.

"Everything's ready for testing, Tom," said Kojo later that afternoon.

"Let's test it for real," said Tom.

"No, no, no!" said Sima. "Absolutely not … N-O-T … NOT!"

"So that's a 'no' then," grinned Tom.

"I agree with Sima," said Kojo. "I don't want to be buried alive in some old cave. No way!"

"Oh, come on, it will be really exciting," said Tom.

"NO!" cried Sima and Kojo together, laughing at Tom's sad expression.

But Tom wasn't going to give up so easily. The next day he came into the office with enough potholing equipment for everyone.

"I've borrowed this gear from Ben," he said. He handed Sima a helmet. "Try it on and then you'll see how safe it would be to play the game for real. The equipment is brilliant. You'll be completely safe."

Sima put on the helmet. Kojo tried on the special boots.

"Well, I suppose the right equipment does make it safer," said Sima.

"Yeah, these boots are amazing," said Kojo.

"And you could build an extra safety feature into the game, Kojo," said Tom. "How about creating something that can stop the game instantly if it gets too dangerous?"

Kojo thought for a few minutes. "I could make a small keypad that controls the game time function," he muttered, as he made some calculations on a notepad. "Yes, I think that's a strong possibility. Give me a couple of hours and I'll get something sorted out."

By the time everyone else had gone home, Kojo had completed the programming and it was time to test the game for real.

They quickly put on all the clothing and equipment that Tom had brought for them.

Then Kojo loaded the game onto his computer.

"Remember," he said, "we must all touch the screen together to enter the game. The game is only finished when we hear 'Game Over'. However, I have the keypad to control the game time. If we are in any danger it will take us straight out of the game. Do you both understand?"

"Yes," said Sima and Tom.

They all touched the screen together. A bright light flashed and they shut their eyes tightly. The bright light faded and they opened their eyes.

CHAPTER 3

Tom, Sima and Kojo were in a dark cave, deep underground.

To begin with the game was really exciting. Sima quickly found some fossils from the scavenger hunt list, and Kojo found a dead bat and the skeleton of a rat. Tom found a small stalactite. They were all really pleased with themselves.

"You might need to add some extra features to this game, Sima," said Tom. "We've found everything on the list already."

"I agree," said Sima. "I thought I'd made it harder than this. I'll tweak the designs when we get back and Kojo can reprogram it."

Sima put the last of the fossils in her backpack and buckled the straps firmly into place. But just then, there was a loud whooshing sound and all three of them felt themselves being hurled down a narrow tunnel.

The tunnel dropped sharply and Sima, Tom and Kojo struggled wildly as they hurtled down into the darkness.

The tunnel opened up into a huge cavern and they fell on the floor in a heap.

"Where are we?" asked Sima as she struggled to her feet.

"Oh no," whispered Tom. "I don't believe it. Look over there."

Sima and Kojo saw three skeletons propped against the far wall of the cavern.

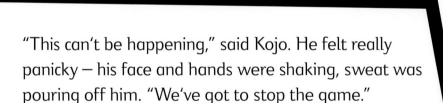

WE MUST BE IN THE BONE BOWL.

"This can't be happening," said Kojo. He felt really panicky – his face and hands were shaking, sweat was pouring off him. "We've got to stop the game."

Kojo fumbled as he got out the keypad from his backpack. Quickly, he pressed the buttons, but nothing happened. He shook it hard and tried again, but still the keypad wouldn't work.

Kojo slumped to the ground. "It's no good," he said. "We're so far underground that the keypad signal won't work. I'm so sorry. I've let you both down. I don't know how we are going to get out of this mess."

Sima and Tom sat down next to him.

IT'S NOT YOUR FAULT. WE'LL SORT SOMETHING OUT.

YEAH, SOMETHING WILL TURN UP.

Just then, they heard someone shouting. Looking up, they saw two men trapped on a cramped ledge, high up on the cavern wall.

"Hey, I recognise them," said Tom. "It's Jed and Ryan from my potholing session! How could they have got into the game? This is surreal."

Sima bit her lip. "Oh no," she said. "I think this is my fault. Do you remember, I used your cave photos, Tom?"

"Yes," said Tom. "But I don't see what that's got to do with it."

"Well, because they were in the photos I scanned, I've made Jed and Ryan part of the game. I didn't mean to," whispered Sima.

"There's nothing we can do about that now," said Kojo. "What we have got to do is help them. Come on."

Sima, Tom and Kojo carefully climbed up to the two men. Then, inch by inch, they helped them to a wider ledge lower down the cavern wall.

"Thanks," said Jed. He looked more closely at Tom. "Don't I know you?"

"Yes," said Tom. "We met at the potholing session at the weekend."

"This is all very weird," interrupted Ryan. "Jed and I were potholing when we suddenly saw this bright light and found ourselves stranded here. We don't remember falling or anything. It's as if we just landed here out of the blue!"

38:00

Tom, Sima and Kojo looked at each other but said nothing.

Ryan looked around the cavern. "We need to get out of here," he said. "But how do we manage that?"

Suddenly, Sima looked up.

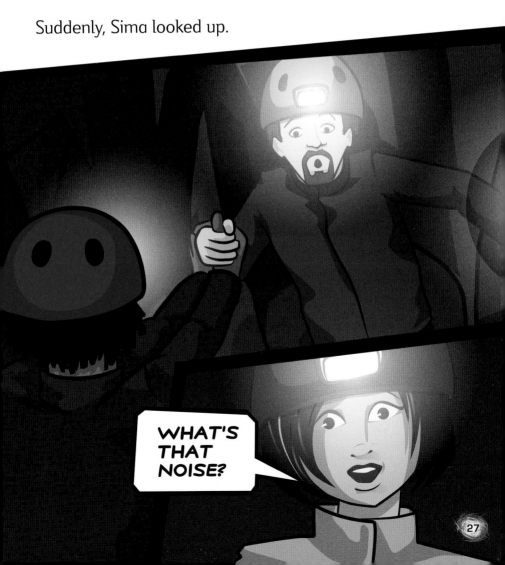

WHAT'S THAT NOISE?

CHAPTER 4

Just then, there was a loud roar and water gushed into the cavern. The water level rose fast. Sima, Tom, Kojo and the two men felt themselves being pushed higher and higher up the sides of the cave until they were pressed hard against the roof. Sima spluttered as she struggled to keep her head above the water.

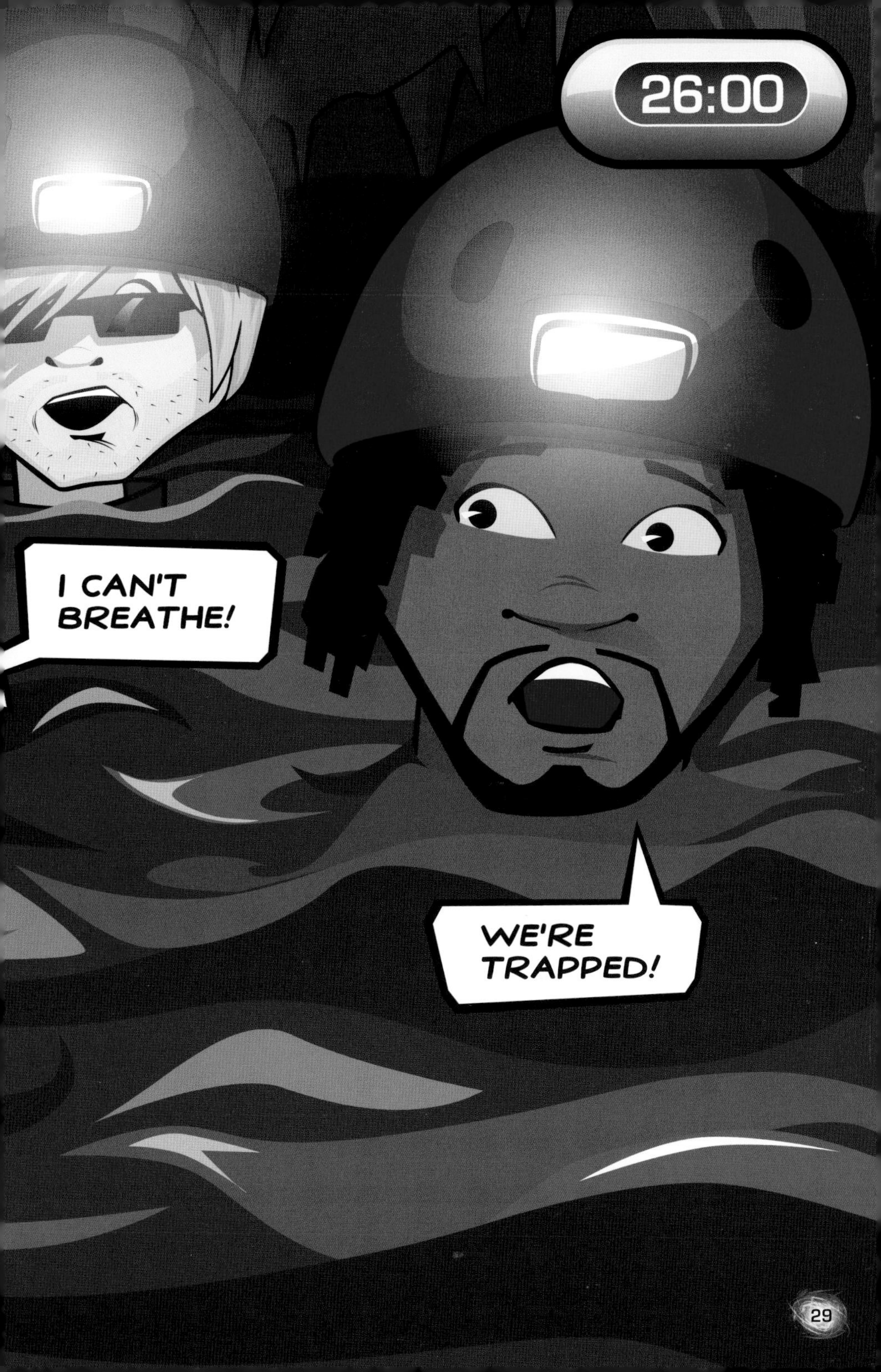
26:00
I CAN'T BREATHE!
WE'RE TRAPPED!

Tom scanned the water and spotted a shaft of light shining on the surface. He searched the roof to see where the light was coming from and noticed a small gap in the rock.

"Look," Tom shouted. "I can see light! That must lead out to the surface."

THAT'S A TINY GAP! WE'LL NEVER SQUEEZE THROUGH THERE.

IT'S OUR ONLY OPTION.

Tom swam towards the small gap and pulled himself onto a narrow ledge underneath. The others followed close behind.

Tom heaved himself out of the water and squeezed his hand into the gap.

"This gap's wider than it looks," he said. "I can feel a boulder blocking the entrance. I think it's some sort of shaft. There seems to be quite a bit of space behind it. If we can move the boulder we might be able to climb to safety."

"But how can we move a boulder?" asked Sima. "We don't have any equipment."

"I've got just the thing," said Jed. He ripped open his backpack and pulled out a small pick axe. He handed it to Tom.

Tom began chipping away at the boulder with the pick axe.

"What good will that tiny axe do?" said Kojo. "It'll take forever to chip the rock away with that."

"Trust me," said Tom, "I know what I'm doing."

Kojo looked at the water level in the cavern. It was nearly over the ledge and rising fast. "I really hope you do know what you're doing," he said, "because things don't look too great from where I'm standing."

Tom chipped hard at the base of the boulder until a deep crack appeared.

Then he pointed to a long, jagged piece of rock lying on the ledge. "Help me push that into the crack."

Kojo, Jed, Sima and Ryan lifted the rock and wedged it into the crack.

"Right," said Tom. "On the count of three I want you all to push down hard on the rock. With any luck, it should lever the boulder out of the way."

ONE
TWO
THREE!

Everyone pushed hard. The boulder creaked and creaked but it didn't move.

"This isn't going to work," cried Sima.

"It will work," insisted Tom. "Push harder!"

Everyone pushed harder. The boulder creaked loudly and then suddenly rolled away.

Tom peered up the shaft. It was very narrow, but it was their only chance.

"Follow me," he ordered. He pushed himself into the gap. The rocks pressed on his chest and he felt as if he couldn't breathe. Slowly, he clawed his way up. He could hear the others close behind him.

Gradually, the shaft widened out, but streams of water cascaded down the walls making it hard to keep a grip as he climbed up.

After a few minutes more, he felt cold air on his face. He heaved himself out of the shaft and fell onto the ground exhausted. Quickly, he sat up and then helped to pull the others to safety. Just as the last person got out, they heard the words 'Game Over'.

WE MADE IT!

A bright light flashed and they shut their eyes tightly.

CHAPTER 5

The bright light faded and when they opened their eyes they were back in the office.

Jed and Ryan looked at each other with their mouths open.

"Would someone mind telling us what's going on?" said Ryan.

"Yes, if this is some kind of a joke ..." began Jed.

"Let me explain," said Tom. "It's like this ..."

"No," interrupted Kojo, "let me explain. You see, it's all to do with this new computer game that we have been developing. Sima designed it and I programmed it, and unfortunately you two have become part of the game. Do you understand?"

The two men sidled towards the door keeping their eyes firmly fixed on Kojo.

"He's crazy," whispered Ryan.

"He sure is," said Jed. "Let's get out of here."

"Please don't worry," said Sima. "Kojo is just teasing. Of course you're not part of a computer game. That would be ridiculous, wouldn't it? Let me call you a taxi and you'll be home before you know it."

Sima picked up her mobile, dialled a number and then smiled at the men. "If you'd like to wait outside the taxi will be here any minute."

The men opened the door and, without saying a word, ran out of the building.

Sima, Tom and Kojo slumped down into their chairs.

"That was the worst game ever," said Sima. "I'm never doing that again."

"I thought it was cool," said Tom.

"You are so weird," sighed Kojo, "if you think that experience was cool!"

Just then Chris Wilson, their boss, came into the office. He had been working late.

"This is becoming something of a habit," he said. "I seem to find you three in the offices after normal working hours more and more often."

He looked at the wet and muddy patches all over the office floor.

"And where has all this mess come from?"
he asked. "It's disgraceful the way you treat
this place. It looks like a pigsty. Clear it up
immediately and then I want you in my office first
thing tomorrow morning with a full explanation
of what you have been up to." And with that, he
slammed the door behind him.

"Ooh, he's a bit grumpy tonight," observed Sima.

"What are we going to tell him tomorrow?" asked
Kojo. "He'll never believe us if we tell him the
truth."

"I suggest that we all go for a takeaway and work
out a different story that he will believe," said
Tom, wringing out his damp socks onto the floor.

"Nice one, Tom," said Kojo.

They turned off the lights and went out of the office.

"In future, Tom," said Sima, as they left the building, "you'll be getting a card and a book from us for your birthday. Do you hear me?"

"Yes, I hear you," sighed Tom. "I hear you loud and clear!"

Glossary of terms

cascade(d) to flow down in large amounts

cave a large hole under the ground

cavern a large cave

equipment the tools or machines you need to do an activity or job

expert someone who knows a lot about a particular subject

fossil an animal, plant or parts of these things that lived long ago and have been preserved in rock

graphics pictures produced by computers

gruesome something that is unpleasant

potholer(s) a person who goes potholing

potholing the sport of going into holes

underground or in mountains

scavenger a game where you hunt for things on a list that have little or no value

souvenir something you buy to remind you of a place you have visited

stalactite(s) a long piece of rock that hangs down from the roof of a cave

stalagmite(s) a long piece of rock that rises up from the floor of a cave

tuition teaching a particular subject

tweak to make minor adjustments to something

voucher an official piece of paper that you use instead of money to pay for a service

Quiz

1 Why did Sima and Kojo give Tom a card?

2 What was the voucher for?

3 Where did they all meet for lunch on Saturday?

4 What was the name of the potholing expert?

5 What sort of hunt was the game based on?

6 Who were trapped in the cavern?

7 Where had Tom met them before?

8 What cascaded into the cavern?

9 How did they all escape?

10 Why was Chris Wilson cross?

ABOUT THE AUTHOR

Sue Graves has taught for thirty years in Cheshire schools. She has been writing for more than ten years and has written well over a hundred books for children and young adults.

"Nearly everyone loves computer games. They are popular with all age groups — especially young adults. But I've often thought it would be amazing to play a computer game for real. To be in on the action would be the best experience ever! That's why I wrote these stories. I hope you enjoy reading them as much as I've enjoyed writing them for you."

Answers to Quiz

1 It was Tom's birthday

2 It was for Tom to go potholing

3 Frankie's Café

4 Ben

5 Scavenger hunt

6 Ryan and Jed

7 At the potholing centre

8 Water

9 Through a gap in the cavern roof that led to the surface

10 Because the office was wet and muddy